SHELDON WEINBAUM

THE AMAZING SCIENTIFIC ADVENTURES OF HARVY, A BRILLIANT CANE

Printed in the United States of America

ISBN   978-1-959483-71-7   (Paperback)
ISBN   978-1-959483-92-2   (Hardback)

Library of Congress Control Number: 2023910521

History
2023.08.07

To my three wonderful grandchildren
Aidan, Amara and Jude.

PREFACE

This book was inspired my grandchildren Aidan, Amara and Jude, who ranged in age from seven to eleven when it was first written. Aidan and Jude called their Grandfather Guya and Amara called him Papa so to accommodate all three grandchildren, Papa/ Guya, is abbreviated as PG throughout the book. PG loved to tell his own children's stories when they were young, but these stories were never written down. Now I will be telling a new story, half fact and half fiction. Most importantly, it will be written down so that when you think of PG, you can tell it to your own children or other children—if they like stories that are half fact and half imagination. The story is about Harvy, PG's devoted and trusted traveling companion, which he takes with him on nearly all his trips, both short and long. Harvy is his cane, a talking cane with childlike qualities, a vivid imagination, and a special curiosity about science. Most of the human elements in the story actually took place. *The paragraphs in italics contain more detailed scientific discussion that can be skipped for the younger child.*

Chapter 1

HOW HARVY AND PG BECAME FRIENDS

There is an old riddle, "What first walks on four legs in the morning, two legs in the afternoon, and three legs in the evening?"

The answer to this is clearly a human being, who first crawls on all fours, then learns after great effort to walk on two legs, and finally has to walk with the aid of a cane. PG had already reached this last stage just before his eightieth birthday and had purchased a handsome cherry-wood cane.

PG was very fond of his beautiful, sleekly polished cane but had not yet chosen a name for his cane. He had even started to talk to his cane, usually comments like, "Where the devil did I leave you?" or, "How could I have left the house without you?" One day PG was in the Brooklyn Botanical Gardens and saw a very friendly older gentleman with a cane whose design was almost the same as PG's. He was using his cane to point out to his female companion a very attractive water fountain.

PG said to this man, "You know, I think our canes may be twins."

The man, quite intrigued by this comment, walked over to PG and said, "Let me introduce you to Martine."

Not to be outdone, PG looked at his cane and noticed to his surprise that inscribed just below the handle were the letters H A R V Y, which PG had never paid attention to before. PG quickly responded, "Martine, let me introduce you to Harvy."

And so it was that Harvy received a name, and that PG started to think of Harvy as a special friend, whom he talked with when he was alone.

2

In the beginning PG took Harvy only on short trips, mostly around the neighborhood, especially when he anticipated stairs. PG did not dread stairs, but he certainly tried to avoid them, like the stairs going up and down the New York City subway. If he dropped Harvy on a steep flight of stairs, it would be embarrassing to have to ask a complete stranger to pick up a cane at the bottom of the stairs. It is one thing to help a child on the stairs but another to help a cane.

One of the nicest things about Harvy was that you don't have to feed a cane. There was no shopping or cooking for a cane. PG usually did not eat with Harvy at his side anyway. PG could easily trip if he tried walking and eating at the same time. Young people can walk and talk on their cell phones at the same time, but you seldom see this with grandpas and grandmas.

Sleeping was another matter. If you were being bumped and thumped on the sidewalk all day, you can imagine how sore Harvy felt at night. However, PG found that it was not comfortable for him and Nana to sleep with a cane between them. A cane is not nearly as soft as a pillow. You can put a dog in a cage next to your bed, but you would never think of putting a cane in a cage, so Harvy often slept between the two front seats of PG's car, where he was often left after they had gone out together. This did hurt Harvy's feelings. However, if Harvy and PG were in the middle of a conversation, PG would take Harvy with him in the elevator to his apartment so that they could continue their conversation and he would spend the rest of the night in PG's apartment.

Chapter 2

HARVY'S FIRST TRIP TO AN AIRPORT, AND GRAVITY

Later in the spring, Harvy was very excited. He was about to go on an airplane for the first time across the entire country, from New York to Seattle, to see PG's granddaughter Amara. There was a lot of suspense and anxiety. What if he was accidentally left behind at security? What if PG got flustered in following all the directions for his luggage and possessions and completely forgot about Harvy?

However, this did not happen, because PG quickly learned that Harvy was indispensable at airports. When PG had Harvy at his side, he was quickly directed to the priority lane and allowed to board the plane before most of the other passengers. PG had a sore knee and back problems, which was why he had purchased Harvy in the first place.

Harvy also noticed only the smallest pets could go into the main cabin of the airplane with the passengers, but any pet that was three feet long would never be allowed in the passenger cabin. A cane had special status, and some canes were even in the first class cabin. However, PG seldom traveled first class.

Harvy had seen planes take off and noticed how they got smaller and smaller as they climbed into the sky. The thought of shrinking as the plane grew smaller was not very appealing.

PG explained that all things looked smaller the farther they are from you, and that any object, no matter how large, would seem like a point at infinity. PG told Harvy to take a look at the moon. Did he realize that the diameter of the moon was actually one-quarter that of the earth, but it was also 240,000 miles away, ten times the distance to circle the earth at the equator? And what about Jupiter, the largest planet in our solar system? It was eleven times the diameter of the Earth, but it was so far away it looked like a tiny dot when compared with the moon.

Harvy was convinced, and his fear of shrinking vanished.

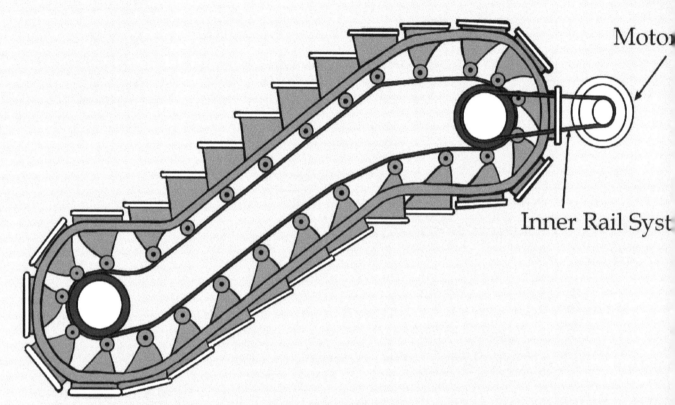

Motor

Inner Rail Syst

Harvy was entranced by the escalators at the airport. He watched the moving stairs and wondered what happened to the stairs when they seemed to disappear into the floor beneath them. He asked PG what happened when the stairs filled up the basement underneath the floor. PG had to explain that the stairs were on a conveyor belt that would just turn around at the bottom beneath the floor and then head right back up in the opposite direction.

Harvy thought this was a very clever invention. He also observed that it was much easier for PG to fall getting on a down escalator than getting on one that was going up. PG told him this was due to a mysterious force called gravity, which acted on all objects large or small, you or the planet Earth on which you stand.

This made sense to Harvy, since he had noticed how hard it as for a baby to learn to stand when she or he was being pulled down by gravity. Harvy was completely intrigued by this mysterious force and asked PG to explain how gravity worked.

PG told Harvy that this great mystery was finally explained by an Englishman, Isaac Newton, who lived more than three hundred years ago. Newton wrote a famous book called *Principia* in which he developed the laws that govern the forces on objects when they accelerate—that is, increase their velocity. This is the distance you go in a unit of time (e.g., meters per second or miles per hour). Acceleration occurs when a car speeds up or a rocket takes off.

Newton also developed the laws of gravitation. By studying the orbits of planets around our sun and orbits of the moons around the planets, Newton was able to show that two bodies always exert a force of attraction on one another, which we call F.

The force F is called a gravitational force and is created by the mass of these heavenly bodies. The force acts through a central point called their center of gravity. Every object, including Harvy, has a center of gravity. PG illustrated this by balancing Harvy on his forefinger and showing that there is just one point where the cane could be perfectly balanced.

PG then explained that the magnitude of F depends on the mass of the heavenly body and the distance you are from its center of gravity. Since planets and their moons are spherical, this distance is just their radius if you are standing on their surface. The force F increases as the radius decreases. This is a big effect, since a twofold decrease in radius will result in a fourfold increase in F goes as the radius squared.

Harvy was most curious about his weight on the moon, since he knew humans had already walked on the moon. He had seen videos of astronauts taking giant steps and jumping high on the moon's surface.

PG told him that the mass of the moon was only a little more than 1 percent, or one-hundredth that of the Earth. Harvy then asked, "Why don't you fly off into space when you jump on the moon, if its mass is so small?"

PG then said, "You forgot that the gravitational force also depends on the distance that you are from the center of gravity of the moon when you are standing on its surface. The radius of the moon is only one thousand miles or only one-quarter that of the Earth, whose radius is four thousand miles. This smaller radius makes the effect of its gravity force sixteen times more powerful than if its radius was the size of the Earth. When you combine the effects of mass and radius, you have one one-hundredth times sixteen or sixteen one-hundredths, which is roughly one-sixth. Thus, your weight on the moon is about one-sixth of that on Earth. This is why when you see astronauts jumping on the moon, they can leap high and take giant steps but not fly off into space."

Harvy then asked about Jupiter.

PG replied, "The mass of Jupiter is a little more than three hundred times that of Earth, so you might think you would be too heavy to take even a single step on Jupiter. However, its radius is also eleven times larger than that of the Earth, so when you stand on its surface you are eleven times farther from its center of gravity than you would be on Earth. If you square eleven, you find that the distance effect is one hundred twenty-one times less powerful than standing on Earth. Combining the effects of mass and distance you have three hundred divided by one hundred twenty-one, which is two point forty-eight. Therefore, you would be about two and a half times as heavy on Jupiter as on Earth.

"Still, it might be hard to walk on Jupiter, since scientists believe its surface is composed of soft dense gases, and perhaps it would feel like walking on soft snow. While the Earth is the largest of the planets with a hard surface, Jupiter is the largest of all the planets. It is also famous for its giant red spot, which astrophysicists believe is a huge storm."

While they were waiting for their plane, Harvy watched many people getting on and off the escalator. He noticed that when you got on at the top, the stairs were nearly flat and then gradually increased in height, and when you got off at the bottom, they gradually decreased in height before becoming flat again. Harvy asked PG why this was so.

PG responded, "You are very observant. Most adults would not even have thought about this."

PG then explained, "If the stairs were to drop immediately when you got on, you would fall, because gravity would have to accelerate you to the same velocity as that of the stairs that are moving down. It would be like jumping. Perhaps this would be fun for children, but not too wise for grandpas. Getting off at the bottom of the escalator, the stairs gradually become level since your downward velocity has to decrease to zero. This way you don't trip and you feel a greater force on your feet, which makes you feel more secure when you get off. You can feel this difference much more easily in a fast-moving elevator when you are going up or down."

When they got seated on the plane, PG said to Harvy, "You know, you are very inquisitive and clever. You are starting to ask questions like a real scientist."

Harvy felt so proud.

Moon

Radius 1080 miles
Mass 7.3 x 10^22 kg
Weight 16lbs

 Earth

Radius 3950 miles
Mass 6 x 10^24 kg
Weight 100lbs.

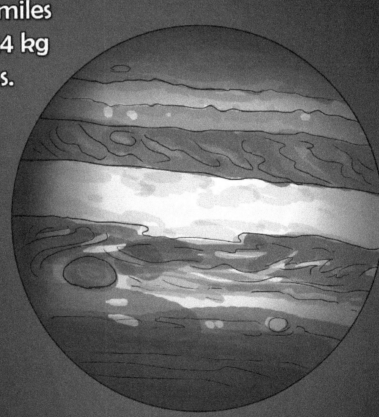

Jupiter

Radius 44,300 miles
Mass 19 x 10^26 kg
Weight 248lbs

Earth, moon and Jupiter

Chapter 3

HARVY'S VISIT TO SEATTLE, AND HIS NEAR-DROWNING EXPERIENCE

Harvy's introduction to his Seattle family was an immediate success. PG's granddaughter, Amara, immediately started dancing with Harvy, swinging Harvy gracefully around doing a dance routine, "One Singular Sensation," from the Broadway musical *A Chorus Line*. Never had Harvy received such attention. Harvy was taken on all family trips in Seattle.

However, there were also moments of great panic. Harvy fell off the dock at a lakeside restaurant during one of Amara's dance routines and nearly drowned. PG's granddaughter came rushing in to tell him that Harvy had fallen into the water and did not know how to float. PG was shocked at this. Harvy, as far as PG knew, was all wood—in fact, beautiful cherry wood.

Everyone knows that wood is lighter (less dense) than water. This defied scientific logic, but seeing was believing. Harvy was for sure at the bottom of the water beneath the dock and not floating. PG hastily brought Matt, Amara's father, to the scene of the accident. Matt was able to get a rake from the groundskeeper, and Harvy was pulled out from the depths. The only lasting evidence of this near-drowning experience was a bruise on Harvy's beautiful handle where a prong from the rake had made a small dent in Harvy's glossy, smooth surface.

PG tried to comfort Harvy after this near-drowning experience. He told Harvy that he also could not float, and for a long time he did not understand why. One day when he was at Imperial College in London on sabbatical, PG had his lung volume measured with a spirometer.

A spirometer is a device that measures the flow of air into and out of your lungs. In an adult male, when you inhale and exhale normally, you take in roughly 0.5 liters of air with each breath. The spirometer can also be used to measure your total lung volume. In this case you

Harvy drowning and screaming for help

breathe in an insert gas (a gas that is not absorbed by your lungs), such as helium or nitrogen. You sit in a closed small room that looks like a telephone booth, and they measure how quickly the concentration of helium or nitrogen increases in the room when you exhale. The rate at which your exhaled helium or nitrogen concentration increases is a measure of your lung volume.

A typical adult male has six liters of air in his lungs (a liter is slightly larger than a quart). However, PG's lung volume was only five liters, a liter less than normal. Since the air in your lungs is what keeps you afloat, PG was less buoyant than most men. In fact, when PG put a small balloon, the size of a quart of milk, in his bathing trunks, he could easily float. This inability to float was a real bonding experience for Harvy and PG, cementing great trust in one another.

Harvy and PG also started to think about experiments they could do to explain why Harvy was also heavier than water.

The rest of this visit to Seattle went very smoothly. However, Harvy's return trip to New York via Washington, DC, was another big adventure, for which PG would be eternally grateful to Harvy. The visit to DC was Harvy's first trip to the National Academy of Sciences, where many famous scientists would meet.

PG trying to float with a small balloon inside his bathing trunks

Chapter 4

HARVY'S VISIT TO THE NATIONAL ACADEMY OF SCIENCES

Harvy's trip to the National Academy of Sciences was initially uneventful. He went to several meetings with PG and was well-behaved. Harvy just observed and never complained when the meetings would drag on. Several of PG's colleagues asked about Harvy, for it was the first time they had met PG's new traveling companion.

Harvy would also join them for meals but never ate. PG would explain that, unlike growing trees, Harvy had stopped growing and needed no nourishment. Harvy liked sleeping by the side of PG's bed in the hotel, which was much more intimate than sleeping between the front seats of PG's car.

The most important event of the trip for Harvy occurred at Reagan Airport on the way back to New York. PG and Harvy were scheduled to fly at 7:00 p.m. that night. By 8:00 p.m. there was no indication that the plane had arrived from New York, and there were heavy thunderstorms all around the airport, much like a grand fireworks display. At 9:00 p.m., there was an announcement that all departing flights would be cancelled and passengers would need to rebook flights for the next morning.

Unfortunately, PG was in the bathroom with Harvy next to him when this announcement was made, and by the time they got out, there were huge lines everywhere with passengers trying to rebook their flights. PG and Harvy saw that there was one counter with an attendant who appeared to be doing nothing.

He looked at Harvy, saw that Harvy had a companion with a disability, and immediately said, "Come with me. This computer is not working. Let's try and find one that is." As luck would have it, the attendant found a working computer at another counter.

He got PG and Harvy on an early flight the next morning and gave them a tip on how to find a hotel near the airport that still had rooms, since nearly all the hotels near the airport were already booked. Harvy and PG felt so happy till they went outside to find

PG and Harvy waiting for a taxi at Reagan Airport

a taxi. Several thousand people had been stranded, and the line for the taxis was as far as the eye could see.

Harvy nudged PG and dragged him to the front of the line, where the dispatcher could easily see them. The dispatcher knew that no one would be annoyed if an old man with a cane for his companion was given special attention. The next taxi was pulled over for them.

When Harvy and PG got to the hotel, they realized that it was a most luxurious hotel. When PG asked what was the price of the room and was told, he nearly fainted. PG and Harvy now knew why this hotel still had rooms for stranded passengers. Harvy then stood up tall in front of the desk so that the concierge could clearly see them.

The concierge said to PG, "I see you have a disability. For airport emergency customers with a disability, the price is only one-third of the regular price."

That night, Harvy and PG went to sleep delighted with their bargain, and as a special reward, Harvy slept in a king-size bed on a pillow right next to PG. After this experience PG vowed to never take a trip without his dear friend Harvy.

Chapter 5

HARVY HAS NIGHTMARES

Harvy and PG returned to New York without further adventures and fell into their usual routine, PG sleeping in his apartment and Harvy in PG's car. Unfortunately, Harvy started to have recurring bad dreams. The dreams were different versions of the same dream, namely about his fears of drowning.

It was clear that his near-drowning experience in Seattle had a more lasting effect. PG offered that Harvy could sleep next to him in his queen-sized bed that night. While this offer was warmly received, it didn't seem to help. Harvy got up in the middle of the night, and neither of them were then able to get back to sleep. This made for very grouchy companions in the morning. PG offered to take Harvy to a sleep therapist, and the offer was quickly accepted.

The therapist, Dr. Sleepberger, was widely recognized in New York for being able to get to the heart of sleep problems stemming from bad dreams.

Harvy on Dr. Sleepberger's couch

After several therapy sessions, Dr. Sleepberger came up with her diagnosis and treatment. She told PG that if Harvy could understand why he was not able to float, he would lose his fear of drowning. After all, in the scientific literature there were only two known woods that were heavier than water, ebony and iron wood, and Harvy was neither of these. Harvy was cherry wood.

Dr. Sleepberger hypothesized that if they could solve this mystery, Harvy's fear of drowning would disappear. After all, PG himself had had bad dreams of drowning until he took the spirometer test at Imperial College and was able to understand why he could not float without a small balloon in his swim trunks. And so it was that PG and Harvy decided to undertake a serious scientific experiment. PG had gotten his PhD in fluid physics and was most receptive to this approach.

PG asked Harvy to read the basic studies by Archimedes, a famous Greek mathematician, physicist, and engineer who lived in the third century BC. Archimedes had not only developed the beginnings of calculus and geometry (two important areas of mathematics) but had also introduced the concepts of buoyancy (the lift force on an object when placed in water) and flotation. Archimedes had figured out how one could take a complexly shaped object like a cane and determine both its density and volume. The story that is told is that Archimedes would sit in his bathtub completely submerged and have his assistant measure how much the water would rise when he got in the tub. This change in height times the area of the tub was his volume, if the tub had the shape of a box. If you do not have an assistant, what you do is fill the bathtub up to the very top with water and then get in. The volume of water than spills on the

floor of the bathroom is then equal to your volume.

This is not an experiment that would make most parents happy. However, you can do this in any shaped tub provided you can collect all the water.

Density is a more subtle concept. It is defined as the weight of an object of a given volume compared to the weight of hte same volume of water. The density of water is assumed to be 1.0, or sometimes stated as weight of water in one cubic centimeter, which is 1.0 gm/cm3. The density of iron is 7, meaning that it is 7 times as heavy as water 7.0 gm/cm3. The density of oak wood is 0.75, meaning that it is only 0.75 times as heavy as water.

Anything that has a density less than 1.0 should float, and if greater than 1.0, it should sink. Archimedes' famous principle states that when you put an object in water, the buoyancy force is equal to the weight of the water it displaces. If this weight is greater than the buoyancy force, it will sink. If this weight is less than the buoyance force, it will float. The buoyancy arises from the water pressure that surrounds the surface of the object.

Cherry wood Density 0.7

Ebony Density 1.2

Two-log experiment to measure density.

In our illustration, you see two logs that look the same and have the same volume. However, the one on the top is cherry wood, whose density is 0.7, and the one on the bottom is ebony, whose density is 1.2. The density of ebony is greater than 1.0, and it sinks. The log on the top floats with 30 percent of its volume above the water's surface. Seventy percent of the log's volume is below the surface, since this is the amount of water that is displaced by the log. The weight of this water, according to Archimedes, is the buoyancy force. The ebony log on the bottom sinks because its density is greater than 1.0, and the weight of the water displaced by the log, its buoyancy force, is less than the weight of the log.

How can one accurately measure the volume of a complex shape like Harvy, who has many beautiful curves? The answer is simple. You do Archimedes' bathtub experiment. You put a very tall vase in a large pan and fill the vase to the very top with water. You then put Harvy very briefly into the water and measure how much water flows out of the vase and into the pan.

When PG suggested this experiment to Harvy, he got very nervous.

He said, "I have been completely submerged in water once, and I am not about to do this again!"

PG then said, "But you only have to do this for one second. Nothing will happen to you."

Harvy then said, "Why don't I submerge you in a vase that is taller than you are and see if you would like it?"

As we all know, fear is sometimes very irrational.

Harvy then said, "Let's see if we can't do a simpler experiment first, where I don't have to risk being drowned. I would rather sacrifice my toe than my entire body."

And so PG removed the rubber tip of Harvy and cut off about one inch of the cane at its tip. This was not pleasant, but losing a toe was far better than being drowned. They then put Harvy's toe in a glass of water to see if it would sink. To their amazement, Harvy's toe could float. Clearly the mystery of Harvy's drowning had not been solved. Cherry wood was clearly less dense than water. Harvy was also now one inch shorter, but he could live with this since he was still significantly taller than most other canes. Furthermore, his handle was his most attractive feature, much like humans, whose most attractive feature is usually their heads and rarely their toes.

Chapter 6

HARVY GETS X-RAYED AND LEARNS WHY HE CAN'T FLOAT

PG and Harvy were shocked when they discovered that Harvy's toe could float, but all of Harvy couldn't. Why was all of Harvy denser than water but Harvy's toe lighter than water?

Harvy then raised a very perceptive question. "PG, aren't the bones in humans heavier than water?"

"Yes," answered PG, "but most humans can float because they are not the same material all over. They have fat and muscle, lungs and bones, and all are of different density, and lungs are filled with air, which weighs hardly anything."

Harvy then replied, "I know I don't have lungs, since I am not aware of breathing, but maybe I have something like bones that are heavier and we just can't see them."

PG thought this was a brilliant insight. Maybe Harvy wasn't all cherry wood after all. Maybe he had a spine like humans, but it just wasn't visible. This would be a difficult experiment to perform, because how can you see through wood?

PG knew Harvy would never agree to be cut in half. What human would ever agree to do this? Harvy had heard there were magicians who claimed they could saw people in half, but everyone knew this was a trick or an illusion. Harvy might agree to have his toe cut off, but to be cut in the middle? *Never.*

PG thought for a while and finally said, "Harvy, I have an idea. You know if you shine a light on paper you can still see through the paper? Look, I will hold my hand behind the paper and you shine the flashlight on the paper and see if you can't see the shadow of my hand. Light waves are only partially blocked by the paper. Paper is made from finely ground wood fibers that stick together after being turned into a watery soup called pulp. Maybe there are some waves that can travel through wood."

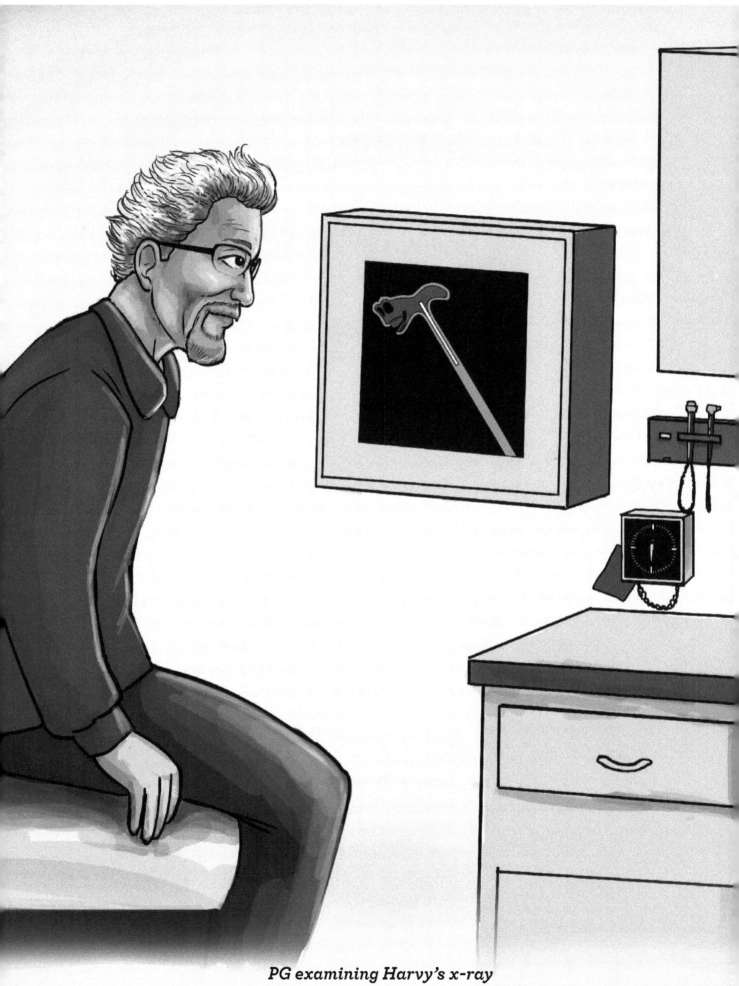

PG examining Harvy's x-ray

Harvy was very excited by this idea. He knew about ocean waves and sound waves but knew very little about light waves.

PG explained that light waves are electromagnetic waves that physicists study. They also study waves that have much higher energy, called x-rays, and that can pen- etrate things that light waves just can't. For example, they can see your bones. Harvy knew you took x-rays to see if you had broken bones, but seeing through your skin and the soft tissue underneath was hardly like seeing through wood. PG said he did not know the answer to this question for sure, but this was why science was so exciting. You ask questions you do not know and hope you will be surprised by the answer.

Electromagnetic waves differ from mechanical waves in that they can travel through a vacuum and even from stars far out in space. Our closest star is our sun, and it takes about eight minutes for the light from our sun to reach us. Sound waves are mechanical waves in that they travel through air, which has many molecules that are far enough apart that you can see right through air. Sound waves are created by the collision if air molecules, and these waves disappear in a vacuum, which has no air molecules. This was demonstrated in a famous experiment where a bell was rung in a jar in which all the air molecules were removed. Once could no longer hear the bell ring.

The next morning PG called his friends at Mount Sinai School of Medicine and told them he would like to take an x-ray of his dear friend Harvy, who was a cherry wood cane. The secretary who answered the phone initially thought PG was joking, but PG persisted. No one in the hospital had ever taken an x-ray of a wooden cane before. Harvy was so excited to be the subject of such a special experiment.

The researchers at the hospital knew PG often had very strange ideas, which sometimes turned out to be true. Harvy was scheduled for x-rays the next day with the proviso that this strange experiment would not be told to any of the clinical doctors, who might scoff at such an absurd use of hospital equipment.

The big day came, and PG and Harvy went to register, claiming that PG was having an x-ray of his leg for his bad knee, which PG told them was covered by his insurance for people who have retired. Clearly no one in their right mind would give health insurance to a wooden cane. This deception worked beautifully, and Harvy and PG were taken to the x-ray room, where no one except PG's research colleagues knew who was being x-rayed.

With great excitement they examined the x-rays, and as Harvy had brilliantly guessed, there was a metal rod in his interior that went from the center of his handle halfway down the center of Harvy's body. Harvy had the equivalent of a spine. Harvy was so pleased with himself and would have puffed out his chest if a wooden cane had a chest. Most important, as Dr. Sleepberger's diagnoses had predicted, Harvy's drowning nightmares vanished.

Harvy had developed a great appreciation for the subtle workings of the mind and the mysteries that could be solved by scientific experimentation.

Chapter 7

HARVY'S VISIT TO THE AIR AND SPACE MUSEUM

Having mastered the mechanics of buoyancy and flotation, Harvy became fascinated by the mechanics of flight. This was inspired by PG's grandchildren, Aidan and Jude in Massachusetts. They were soccer fanatics, much like PG had been a baseball fanatic when he worshiped the old Brooklyn Dodgers. However, it was hard for Harvy to play soccer, since he had only one leg. It was Aidan's and Jude's interest in the world of Legos, especially Lego sets from which you could build jet planes, rockets, and spaceships, that captured Harvy's attention.

This interest was reinforced when Harvy learned that PG had actually worked with several well-known aerospace companies in the early part of his career, when humans were first trying to go to the moon. PG had had done research on supersonic flight and the reentry of space vehicles into the Earth's atmosphere from outer space.

Harvy had become a keen observer of bird flight because PG had a vacation home in Woodstock with a pond, where many waterfowl came to visit. Harvy believed, just like humans had for centuries, that one could fly if one could imitate bird flight. However, he had already been to several airports and had yet to see any airplanes that flapped their wings. Even more amazing, at PG and Nana's country house were humming birds, who could defy gravity entirely by fluttering their wings without moving their bodies. PG told Harvy that he was a keen observer and was asking just the right questions.

Shortly thereafter, a great opportunity arose to explore these questions. Aidan and Jude had already visited the Air and Space Museum in Connecticut and proposed that they go with PG and Nana to this museum, where some of the great pioneers of aerospace were honored. One could also closely examine their flying machines.

Of special interest was the helicopter designed by the great helicopter pioneer Igor Sikorsky. Dr. Sikorsky was born in Kiev, a Russian city, where PG's father had gone to engineering school. The museum specialized in early aircraft, including Sikorsky's helicopters. Everyone was so excited by this proposed trip.

To enter the museum, you had to go through a metal detector at the entrance. No one had any trouble until Harvy tried to pass and a screeching alarm went off. The guard immediately told Harvy to stop and examined the cane with careful scrutiny. PG told the guard that Harvy was his dear companion and that the cane had a metal spine in its interior, which could not be seen from the outside but could be seen in x-rays. The guard said he could only see what he could see and rules were rules. Only when PG brought Harvy's x-rays to his superior, and he received her approval, would things change. Until then, Harvy would need to be checked at the entrance.

PG explained that this was a large museum with lots of walking, and he could not do this without Harvy, his trusted and loyal cane. PG told the guard that if he did not allow Harvy to pass, it would spoil the entire family outing and would be extremely disappointing to his grandchildren. They had come specially to see the new exhibit on virtual flying using videos.

After much pleading by Aidan and Jude, Harvy was allowed to enter. PG told the guard that Harvy was a brilliant cane and had come to the museum specially to try and understand how planes and helicopters could fly without having wings that flapped or bodies that hovered without moving. The guard was truly puzzled. He had never thought of these very basic questions before.

Much of what Harvy had learned about flying had come from watching ducks take off and land on PG's pond in Woodstock. Harvy knew there was something miraculous about air. Even though air was invisible and you could look right through it, you could easily feel air, especially on a windy day. PG told Harvy that the force of the wind on any object in its way was called pressure. It also didn't seem to matter who was moving, whether you were stationary and the wind blew past you, or you were moving, as on a bicycle, and there was no wind.

Harvy also noticed that when the ducks landed, they did not have to flap their wings at all. Landing was very graceful and almost effortless. They simply glided to a stop and slowed their landing with their webbed feet. Take-off was another matter and required a lot of work. They furiously flapped their wings, and since there were tall trees all around PG'S pond, the ducks had to fly in circles around the pond to fly high enough before finding an opening so they didn't crash into the trees.

Harvy noticed that when the ducks first took off, the surface of the water was greatly disturbed beneath their wings. Clearly every time they flapped their wings, the presssure beneath their wings was also felt on the water below. Harvy, being a very clever cane, realized that the pressure beneath their wings was what lifted them up. PG told Harvy that humans had tried attaching wings to their arms, and all such experiments had ended in failure and in some cases broken bones.

Harvy was also puzzled by the observation that once the ducks got themselves in the air, they could only fly forward and never backward. This clearly was important, since ducks do not have eyes in the back of their heads and like humans, cannot turn their necks fully around like an owl. Then one day the answer suddenly came to Harvy. The pressure force under their wings was not just upward (which scientists call lift) but also forward (which scientists call thrust).

The other flying creature that fascinated Harvy was the hummingbird. Unlike ducks, who only moved forward when they were flying, hummingbirds seemed to defy gravity and when eating the sweet contents (nectar) of a flower, could hover without moving at all. How could one maintain lift without moving? This seemingly impossible behavior gave rise to humans inventing the helicopter, a vehicle that had no wings at all.

Harvy would stare at the wings of the hummingbird, but they moved so quickly it was a blur. When PG realized this, he told Harvy that someone had taken very fast videos of hummingbirds hovering and had observed that after every downstroke of its wings, the wings would rotate, much like humans turn their wrist, and the upstroke would become a downstroke and also produce lift.

Harvy was intrigued that nearly all of the early airplanes had two wings, not one on each side like birds, but one on top of the other. These planes were called biplanes, and none of these human-made planes had wings that could flap up and down. The mystery was, how could a wing like this produce lift? This was beyond Harvy's imagination, and he asked PG to explain the exhibit that showed how this was possible.

PG explained in very simple terms that one has to design a wing in such a way that the air flowing over the top of the wing has a lower or negative pressure than the air flowing beneath the wing. A wing whose shape was the same on the bottom as on the top and not tilted (zero angle of inclination) would produce no lift no matter how fast it moved. However, if you tilted the wing up even slightly, you would generate lift since the pressure below the wing would increase and the pressure above the wing would decrease.

In our illustration, we have sketched how the pressure above and below the wing changes as the angle of inclination increases. The outward-facing arrows on top of the wing point upward, indicating a negative pressure (less than atmospheric), whereas the arrows below the wing point upward toward the surface, indicating a positive pressure (greater than atmospheric). Note also that this difference increases as the angle of inclination increases.

The difference in pressure just described depends on the velocity of the air passing above and below the wing. The relation between velocity and pressure along a streamline (the path of a tiny element of air flowing either above or below the wing) is related by an equation derived by Daniel Bernoulli nearly three hundred years ago. According to this equation, the velocity of the element of air would speed up when going above the wing, and the pressure would decrease, whereas the air would slow down when it went below the wing and the pressure increased. This difference in pressure created lift without any need to have flapping wings.

In the bottom of the illustration, we show the forces on the wing when the pressures all around the wing are summed up. The sum of all the vertical components of the pressure are called the lift, and the sum of all the horizontal components of the pressure are called the drag due to pressure. There is also drag due to friction. The lift has to support the weight of the airplane, and the drag due to pressure and friction has to be balanced by the thrust from the plane's engines to maintain its speed.

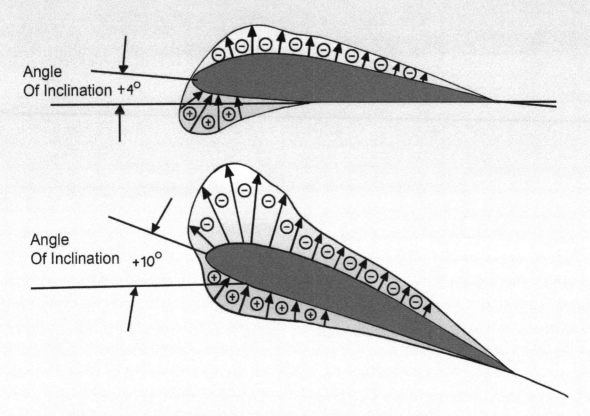

Angle Of Inclination +4°

Angle Of Inclination +10°

"Pressure Distribution Above and Below the Wing."

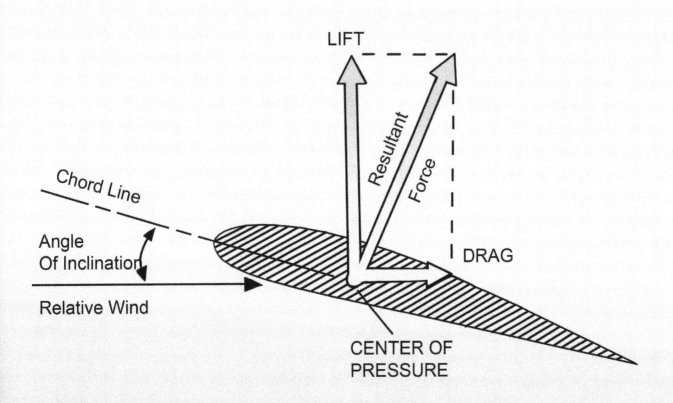

LIFT

Resultant Force

Chord Line

Angle Of Inclination

Relative Wind

DRAG

CENTER OF PRESSURE

"Lift and Drag Force Diagram for Wing"

Harvy was fascinated by the models of the early biplanes and the story of the Wright brothers. The Wright brothers had figured out how to build their own light- weight engine that could turn a propeller to provide sufficient thrust for their biplane to rise off the ground and move forward. In their first successful powered flight in Kitty Hawk in 1903, their plane flew roughly the length of two soccer fields and reached a height of approximately twenty feet. Harvy thought that some humans were really quite clever. They had figured out how to make engines do work they could not do themselves, something ducks could never do.

Harvy was most puzzled when he saw the early helicopters. They had no wings at all, only giant narrow blades that looked like propellers, except that you could change their angle at the center of the shaft about which they were turning. When the blades rotated, they acted like long, slender wings, and this is what produced the lift. By tilting the giant rotor, you could move in any direction, unlike an airplane, which could only fly forward or turn.

The first helicopter that Harvy saw had two sets of rotating blades, one above the other, and they rotated in opposite directions. At first Harvy could not understand why one would want to do this since one blade seemed to be working against the other. PG had to explain that the friction on the rotor would cause the body of the helicopter to turn in circles and the passengers would become very dizzy if this were to happen.

There were two solutions to this very difficult problem. One either needed two sets of blades rotating in opposite directions to balance one another or another smaller rotor blade at the tail to stop the spinning. This is the solution Dr. Sikorsky had proposed, and the one that is now most commonly used. Harvy was beginning to realize how clever the hummingbird was. It had figured out how to hover without turning in circles, which clearly would make eating nectar and insects very difficult.

Harvy was thrilled to have finally understood the principles of human flying, but the most lasting impression was that humans had made great efforts to fly and hover to do things that birds and ducks do naturally. When he thought about it, he realized that humans were slow learners but did a lot of talking. It took humans a year to learn to walk. A little bird, when it pecked its way out of its shell, could walk in a few days. The same was true of ducks, and they all had just two feet. Harvy also realized that birds and ducks learn in much the same way as a baby learns to walk. They try to learn to fly without making serious mistakes that would break their bones.

When Harvy got home, PG showed him videos of hummingbirds to see how they learned to hover without dangerous accidents. For several days they would hold on tight to the bottom of their nest with their tiny claws to be sure they could support their weight when they flipped their wings. By two weeks after hatching from their eggs, they had figured out how to hover.

Ducklings were not as cautious. Harvy watched videos of ducklings learning to fly. They would jump off a low wall and flap their wings to soften the jump when they hopefully landed on their feet. Flying took a lot of practice. By two months, when they were nearly fully grown with feathers, they were able to fly away from home for the first time. Humans, on the other hand, need far more practice to fly planes safely, and only true experts can fly a complicated flying machine like a helicopter.

Chapter 8

HARVY'S EXPERIMENTS WITH SNOW

Harvy, like most children, loved snow, especially big snows where school would be closed. All the children would then be home, and Harvy could watch the children sledding, skiing, and snowboarding in the park. Harvy was especially excited about the possibility of snowboarding. Harvy reasoned that in snowboarding you didn't need poles like in skiing, and PG could still hold on to his cane. PG told Harvy that he was a poor skier even before he needed to walk with a cane and had never snowboarded, but that he did have an old toboggan and he would be happy to take Harvy on his toboggan the next big snowfall.

Harvy couldn't wait, and on the next big snowfall, PG took Harvy to his country house in Woodstock where there were plenty of hills. The big snow day came, and PG found the old toboggan, which he had used forty years ago with his own children. They found the perfect hill for their first trial. They got on the toboggan at the top and must have glided over a thousand feet before they came to a stop at the bottom of the hill. Harvy found the first run exhilarating, like riding on air, but it was so much work for PG to pull the toboggan to the top of the hill again, even when leaning on Harvy all the way to the top.

Harvy said to PG it felt almost like flying.

On the way back to the top of the hill, Harvy noticed something very strange when he looked at the toboggan track. At the bottom of the hill, where the toboggan had ended the ride, their track was almost a foot deep. The same thing was true at the top of the hill when they first got on the toboggan, but on the way down, where they had been traveling the fastest, the snow was barely compressed.

Harvy said to PG, "Do you think we were really flying?" PG said to Harvy, "What do you mean?"

Harvy replied, "Isn't there air in the snow? Maybe the air can't leave quickly enough at the sides of the toboggan when we are moving fast. The snow is soft and fluffy and surely cannot support the weight of the toboggan with us on it, so it must be the pressure of the air that is trapped in the snow below the toboggan that is keeping us up. We are flying like an airplane on the surface of the snow."

PG was amazed that Harvy had such a clever insight. Harvy then asked, "How quickly were we moving?"

PG replied, "Maybe at our fastest we were going about thirty feet per second (twenty miles per hour)."

Harvy then said, "Our toboggan is six feet long, about twice my height." Harvy, who had already become very good at multiplication and division, then said, "It would take only one-fifth of a second to go six feet, and therefore, if the air could not escape from beneath the toboggan in one-fifth of a second, we should be flying. Can we do an experiment where we can measure how quickly air escapes from snow?"

PG replied, "What a wonderful idea. You are now thinking like the Wright brothers and Igor Sikorsky."

Harvy was so excited. Would it be possible to design an experiment where they could measure how quickly air escaped from snow? PG told Harvy there were special instruments called pressure transducers that could take pressure measurements in a small fraction of a second.

A pressure transducer is a device that measures the pressure of air. Air pressure is the force of air on a unit area such as a square foot or a square inch. Atmospheric pressure is the weight of a column of air all the way to the top of the earth's atmosphere. If this column were one square inch in area, it would weigh 14.7 pounds, so the atmospheric pressure where we stand on the ground is 14.7lbs/in2. You don't feel this pressure because it surrounds your entire body, and according to Archimedes, the buoyancy force on your body, which is the weight of the air that your body displaces, is at most a few ounces.

However, you can do a very simple experiment to show that this air pressure is indeed present. Take a glass and fill it with water, and place a thin sheet of plastic or cardboard on top of the glass. Then, quickly invert the glass, being careful to not let the water leak out of the glass and let air enter. You will be surprised to see when you remove your hand from the plastic sheet, the water in the glass will be suspended in mid-air, supported but the atmospheric pressure beneath the plastic sheet.

In contrast to our experiment with the inverted glass, the pressure on the bottom of the toboggan comes from both the air trapped beneath the toboggan and the pressure of the snow crystals. To measure just the air pressure, there is a tiny hole in the surface of the pressure-measuring device that allows only the air and not the snow crystals to enter. When the snow is slightly compressed, most of the pressure comes from the air, since the air is being forced to flow through the tiny pores in the snow crystals. As the air escapes and the snow compresses, most of the pressure will come from the snow crystals. When the toboggan is ten square feet and supports a weight of two hundred pounds, the pressure underneath it would be two hundred divided by ten or $20lbs/ft2$.

Harvy then replied, "Why don't we make a giant snow cake in a container that looks like a giant pot, whose diameter was the same as the width of the toboggan (twenty inches)? The top of the pot has a lid with pressure transducers on its underside (see illustration), and the side walls have the shape of a circular cylinder made of a metal screen. This way the air can easily escape to the outside when a weight is placed on the lid."

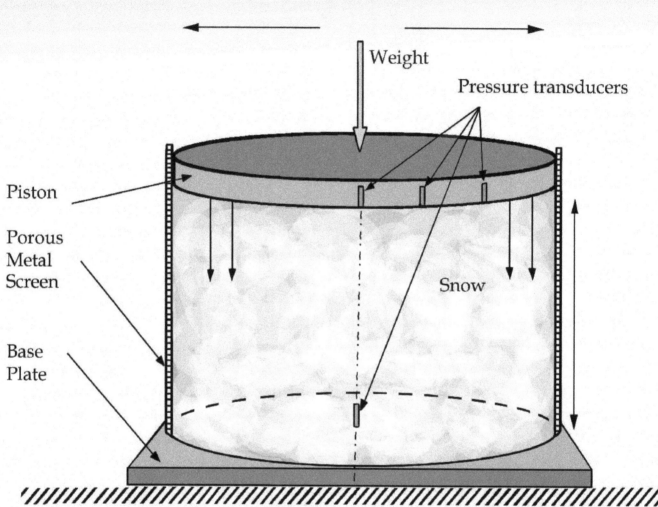

PG said, "This is a great idea." As far as he knew, no one had ever measured how quickly air escaped from snow in the time it took a ski, a snowboard, or a toboggan to move a distance equal to their length, which Harvy had already estimated as one-fifth of a second.

The experiment seemed like such a simple idea. Many of the best ideas are simple. Their toboggan had an area of ten square feet. The area of the lid for their snow cake was about two square feet or about one-fifth the area of their toboggan. Therefore, if PG, Harvy, and the toboggan weighed two hundred pounds, the weight they needed to put on their lid would be about one-fifth of two hundred or forty pounds. The height of their snow cake would be nearly the same as the depth of the snow. Harvy hypothesized that the air should escape from their giant snow cake at nearly the same rate as it escaped from beneath their toboggan.

PG explained to Harvy that he made theoretical models to design experiments, like the snow cake experiment described above, but he was not an experimentalist. An experimentalist is someone who actually builds an experimental apparatus to test whether the predictions of a theoretical model are correct. However, he had a good friend, Yiannis, at the college who was an experimentalist who would love to explore Harvy's idea about toboggans and snowboards flying on snow. And so it was that the experiment sketched in the illustration was built and tested.

The results of the snow cake experiment were very exciting. The air did escape from the giant snow cake, and they could actually observe how quickly the lid descended. At the end of the experiment, after all the air had been pushed out of the cake through the circular sidewall screen, the lid rested quietly on the snow and no longer moved. The height of the cake at this time was about one-third its original height.

The important result was that it took nearly a second for this to happen. This was much longer than the one-fifth of a second that Harvy had estimated their toboggan would cover the snow beneath it if it were moving thirty feet per second. They indeed were flying on air but only one foot off the ground, a different concept than airplanes, which fly several miles up in the sky.

PG was right. No one had ever done an experiment like this, and PG encouraged Harvy to submit their experiment to a prominent science journal. He even told Harvy he would do all the typing and drawing of the figures if Harvy dictated the content of the paper.

Harvy's paper was highly praised by the journal reviewers. It was the first time a cane had ever published a paper in an important scientific journal. Harvy was extremely proud but not yet famous, since no one realized Harvy was a cane. PG and his friend Yiannis, the experimentalist, who were coauthors on the paper, kept this a secret.

Chapter 9

FROM TOBOGGANS TO TRAINS THAT FLY

These experiments with snow were so thrilling that they kept Harvy awake at night thinking. Harvy dreamed of becoming a great aviation inventor like the Wright brothers and Igor Sikorsky. How could Harvy use what was learned from these snow experiments to fly only one foot off the ground? Could you have a floating train without wheels? Indeed, in one of Harvy's dreams, he had a vision that perhaps a large toboggan could lift much greater weights and perhaps carry many passengers.

One night Harvy woke up from sleep with a sudden realization. Toboggans were great and gave you a gloriously smooth ride, but the air in the snow did escape quickly, and then you could no longer float on the trapped air because the air was escaping at the sides of the toboggan. But what if the toboggan glided in a channel filled with snow where air could not easily escape at its sides? Harvy also wondered why you even needed snow at all. Why not use any soft, fluffy material, like feathers or fiber fill used in pillows?

The next morning, as soon as Harvy awoke and saw PG, Harvy told him these new ideas. Instead of a jet plane that had to use so much energy to climb to cruising altitude, why not have a train with a giant ski that flew in a channel on a bed of fiber fill covered by a protective screen? Most importantly, the walls of the channel had to be just a little wider than the width of the ski so that the air could not easily escape, but the channel had to be wide enough so that the ski could easily glide through the channel without scraping the walls. Also, the ski had to be flexible at its sides so that one could make turns.

PG said, "Let's go on a shopping trip to a big pillow store and try lots of different pillows to find one whose fiber-fill is just right."

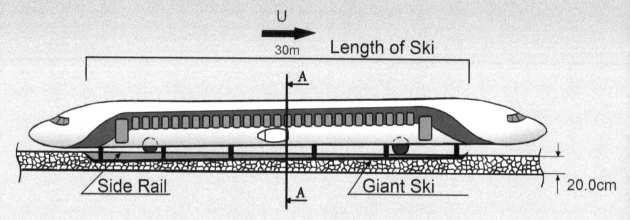

U
30m

Length of Ski

A

Side Rail   Giant Ski

20.0cm

A

Starting Position for Jet Ski Train

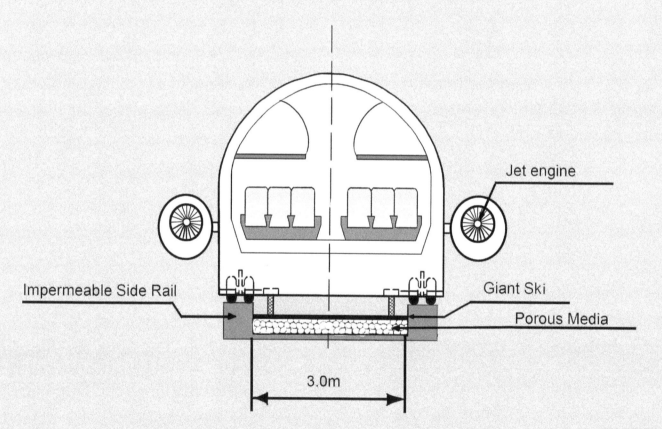

Jet engine

Impermeable Side Rail   Giant Ski

Porous Media

3.0m

Cross Section A-A of Jet Ski Train

Moreover, the pillow had to be able to restore itself. It could not be like snow, which, once compressed, could not expand again. Fortunately, they soon discovered that nearly all the fiber-fill pillows in the store had this self-restoring property, and they were much cheaper than feather pillows.

Harvy then asked how, with so many pillows to choose from, you could decide which pillow was just the right one. PG suggested that just like they made a giant cake of snow they could make a giant cake of fiber-fill using the same test apparatus they had used for snow. All they had to do was measure how quickly the air would escape. Harvy and PG bought lots of pillows for their experiment and spent many hours testing their fiber-fill until they found the pillow that seemed just right.

Harvy was a step ahead of PG. He told PG that they still had to tackle another big problem. A toboggan could just slide down a hill to get started, but a jet train on a giant ski would need a very big hill to get started. Harvy reasoned that his train had to take off like an airplane. Even if it could fly at a height of only one foot off the ground on its fiber-fill bed, it had to get to this height in the first place. Harvy had noticed that even the toboggan did not seem to be floating on air until it reached a certain speed where the air pressure underneath the toboggan would be sufficient to lift it off the ground.

How fast would Harvy's jet ski train have to go before it could float on the air trapped in the fiber fill underneath its giant ski?

PG realized that Harvy had asked a very important and difficult question. PG told Harvy that to answer this very difficult question, he would ask his PhD student, Parisa, to make a mathematical model with many equations that would have to be solved on a computer with a large memory. Such models were very helpful before undertaking experiments that could be very expensive and still fail.

Having found what Harvy and PG thought was the perfect fiber-fill pillow, they went to see their experimental colleague, Yiannis. They discussed with Yiannis the design of a laboratory scale model that was a small version of the full-scale jet ski train that people hopefully would use one day. The model they would need to build would be about one meter long and fly in a fiber-filled channel that was small enough to fit in Yiannis's basement laboratory.

Chapter 10

HARVY BECOMES FAMOUS, AND THE JET SKI TRAIN IS CELEBRATED

Every day the excitement was building as the laboratory model was nearing completion. Harvy could do without sleep, but this wasn't something his human companions could do without. Meanwhile, Parisa's mathematical computer model made two amazing predictions. First, the model predicted that a full-scale jet ski train weighing seventy tons with two hundred passengers could do without wheels and start flying one foot off the ground at a speed of only five meters per second (18 km/hr or 11 miles/hr), about half as fast as a human can run.

Quite remarkably, the model predicted that at this speed, the pressure due to the air trapped beneath the giant ski would be just sufficient to support the entire weight of the jet ski train. The wheels, when no longer needed, could be retracted just like an airplane's after takeoff. However, there was a huge advantage. Big jet planes with two hundred passengers lift off the ground at speeds of 275 km/hr or 170 miles/hr and need runways three thousand meters long to reach these speeds. Harvy's jet ski train could take off in less than one hundred meters.

The second amazing prediction of Parisa's computer model was that Harvy's jet ski train, once airborne, could achieve a cruising velocity of 700 km/hr in less than three minutes. Also, it needed only ten thousand pounds of thrust from its jet engines to achieve this velocity when gliding at the top of its fiber layer, which was only one foot high. Jet planes with two hundred passengers need powerful jet engines with fifty thousand pounds thrust to lift them off the ground and don't achieve cruising velocity and cruising altitude for twenty to thirty minutes, since they have to lift themselves five miles into the sky.

In addition, Harvy's jet ski train could go twice as fast as existing high-speed trains in Europe, China, and Japan. Harvy's insights were an inspiration to the entire team.

Finally, when the laboratory model was completed and instrumented with pressure transducers, the team was able to convincingly demonstrate that their small laboratory model train was actually flying on air trapped in a thin layer of soft fiber fill.

The team was faced with a difficult dilemma. Who would believe that such a project was conceived of by a cane—a truly extraordinary cane? The truth would have to come out that Harvy was a cane. Like their previous paper, Harvy would sign the paper as just Harvy and hopefully no one would ask questions. They sent the paper to a famous physics journal. The paper received exceptional reviews, and the reviewers made flattering comments about its creativity. However, unlike the first paper on air escaping from a cake of snow, this paper was reported on by many other scientific journals because of its potential significance for changing the future of high-speed train travel.

The word spread quickly and was picked up by newspapers and the media. Everyone wanted to meet Harvy, who was very shy and did not like publicity. PG took many of these inquiries and had to explain that Harvy was a cane—an extraordinary cane. Many of the callers would then just hang up in disbelief, but a few would persist and ask PG if he could arrange interviews. Harvy finally consented and agreed to give radio interviews that children and any other talking canes could understand. Some of these interviews were aired in faraway places like Europe, China, and Australia. Newspaper articles would appear with titles like, "Engineers Predict a Future with High-Speed Trains That Fly on Fluff."

One day Harvy received a special letter. It was from Martine, the cane who looked just like Harvy who Harvy had met at the Brooklyn Botanical Garden. It was the beginning of what would become a famous friendship in the world of canes, where Harvy had become an international celebrity. PG would see to it that Harvy and Martine would often get together. Martine, like Harvy, had become enamored by the world of science after being introduced to Parisa, the PhD student who had made the sophisticated computer models for Harvy's jet ski train.

Harvy's dream was that his jet ski train would one day be built and improve the lives of all who would use it. It takes a long time for dreams to be realized, but one day when you are much older, you may ride on a jet ski train. You can tell your own children the story of Harvy, the remarkable cane, who first came up with the idea of a flying train that glides on a track filled with fluff at speeds approaching that of jet planes.

Harvy and PG would continue their adventures for many years, always finding something new and exciting to learn. They found out that there is no ending to all the amazing things that people can learn about everything that surrounds them.

Both adults and children have beloved objects that, if they could speak, could tell you of their lives. Perhaps you, the reader, also have a story to tell about the adventures and mysteries of ordinary things for others that are very special for you in your own life. This could be your bicycle, your roller blades, your binoculars, or things that you have spent many hours building or collecting. If you do, PG and Harvy would love to hear from you.

APPENDIX: THE ACTUAL STORY OF THE JET SKI TRAIN

For those interested in the more scientific aspects of the jet ski train, and to recognize the efforts of PG's former graduate students who worked so hard on this project, I will briefly describe the real story of how the jet ski train came into being. I have listed at the end of this appendix some of the key papers that were instrumental in the genesis of the initial concept, which was biological in origin, and how this concept quite remarkably got transformed into a new idea for a high-speed train. In real life, PG is a biomedical engineer, fluid physicist, and applied mathematician who develops theoretical models to solve mysteries and explore new hypotheses. It will be obvious from this short summary that there is a remarkable cross-fertilization of ideas that comes from interdisciplinary approaches that combine the biological and physical sciences. The initial problem that PG was interested in was how red blood cells could flow through your smallest blood vessels, your capillaries, with very little friction to minimize the work your heart has to do in pumping your blood throughout your entire body. Red blood cells are highly flexible biconcave discs eight μm in diameter (one μm is one-thousandth of a mm) and constitute 40 percent of your blood volume. Your smallest capillaries are only five μm in diameter so that the red cells have to roll up into a bullet-like shape to squeeze through your capillaries. To do this, red blood cells must be very flexible, and they are because they are filled with a fluid called hemoglobin and do not have a nucleus.

Despite the absence of a nucleus, red cells have a membrane that tries to unfold, and one would think this would cause a lot of friction if they would scrape along the membranes of the endothelial cells that form your capillary tubes. The reason this does not happen is that the inner lining of your capillaries has a very thin coat of fibers filled with water called an endothelial glycocalyx. This glycocalyx prevents the membranes of red blood cells and endothelial cells from touching one another unless the red cells have stopped moving. When this happens, the glycocalyx collapses as the water is drained from the fiber layer. The biological functions of the endothelial glycocalyx are described in [1,2].

In 2000, PG proposed that the red cells were actually skiing on the glycocalyx, provided they were moving fast enough to not let the water escape from the fiber layer [3]. Furthermore, the mathematical model showed the same thing would happen for a human skiing on snow, except that you could never be as good a skier as a red cell because the pressure that builds up in the trapped air under your skis would escape at the edges of your skis, whereas a rolled-up red cell is nearly entirely encircled by the endothelial cells surrounding it. To prove this idea, PG hired an expert skier to ski down a slope after a fresh snowfall. The skier then came back and stepped in her ski tracks and sank much deeper into the tracks she had just made. It was clear that much of the weight of the skier and her skis was supported by the air trapped in the snow, and the depth of the ski track depended on how quickly the skier was moving, much like the toboggan in chapter 7 of our story.

In 2005, PG and his colleagues wanted to measure just how quickly air did escape from snow and actually performed the experiment described in chapter 8 on the compression of a snow cake [4]. These results were subsequently used to determine the lift provided by the air trapped in snow when skiing or snowboarding as a function of your speed [5].

The idea that you could greatly enhance your lift when skiing if you could eliminate the loss of air at the edges of the ski, by putting the ski in a channel with impermeable sidewalls, was first proposed in [6]. This paper received widespread attention because the theoretical model predicted you could support a train car weighing fifty tons with one hundred passengers on a giant ski using soft, porous materials similar to goose down, provided the loss of air at the edges of the ski could be mostly eliminated. The key experiments to find an inexpensive soft, porous material with these properties that could restore itself after compression were first reported in [7], and the actual performance of a jet ski train with two hundred passengers weighing seventy tons is theoretically predicted in [8].

The four PhD students who did much of this work are Jerry Feng, Parisa Mirbod, Mia Mia Thi, and Qianhong Wu. All the experiments related to the jet ski train were conducted under the supervision of my collaborator, Professsor Yiannis Andreopoulos. It is the dream of the entire research team that high-speed train travel will one day become a reality, that these concepts will be brought to fruition.

SUGGESTED FURTHER READING:

1. Weinbaum, S., Zhang, X., Han, Y., Vink, S., Cowin, S.C., "Mechanotransduction and Flow Across the Endothelial Glycocalyx," PNAS 100, 7988–7995 (2003).

2. Weinbaum, S., Tarbell, M. J., Damiano, E. R., "The Structure and Function of the Endothelial Glycocalyx Layer," Annu. Rev. Biomed. Eng., 9, 121–167, (2007).

3. Feng, J., Weinbaum, S., "Lubrication Theory in Highly Compressible Porous Media: The Mechanics of Skiing from Red Cells to Humans," J. Fluid Mechanics, 422, 281–317, (2000).

4. Wu, Q., Andreopoulos, A., Xanthos, S., Weinbaum, S., "Dynamic Compression of Highly Compressible Porous Media with Application to Snow Compaction." J. Fluid Mech. 542, 281–304 (2005).

5. Wu, Q., Igci, Y., Andreopoulos, Y., Weinbaum, S., "Lift Mechanics of Downhill Skiing and Snowboarding." Medicine and Science in Sports and Exercise, 1132– 1144 (2006).

6. Wu, Q., Andreopoulos, Y. and Weinbaum, S., "From Red Cells to Snowboarding to a New Concept for Train Track," Physical Review Lett., 93, 194501-1-4 (2004).

7. Mirbod P., Andreopoulos Y., Weinbaum S., "On the Generation of Lift Forces in Random, Soft Porous Media," J. Fluid Mech., vol. 619, 147166 (2009).

8. Mirbod, P., Andreopoulos, Y., Weinbaum, S., "Application of Soft Porous to a High-Speed Train Track," J. Porous Media, 12, 1037–1052 (2009).